Finding
BUNNY

By Renee Bolla

Illustrations by Jess Bircham

Elle loved Bunny.
Bunny was her best friend.
They did everything together.

Elle and Bunny played hide-and-seek and dress-up.

Sometimes they had tea parties and invited Doggy and Teddy.

But their favorite thing to do was snuggle.

When Elle was happy,
Bunny was there to snuggle.

When Elle was sad,
Bunny was there to snuggle.

When Elle got a boo-boo,
Bunny was there to snuggle.

But all the playing and all the snuggling made Bunny a little stinky.

"I think Bunny needs a bath," Mommy said.

"No! I don't want to be away from Bunny," Elle said.

Later that afternoon Mommy left to run a few errands.

"Have a fun day with Daddy!" she said.

Daddy and Elle sat down for lunch.

"Where is Bunny?" she asked.

"I'm not sure, kiddo," Daddy said.

Elle wondered, "Maybe Bunny went to play with friends?"

But she knew Bunny wouldn't go play without her,
so she began to search.

She checked in her playroom,
no luck.

She checked in her closet,
no luck.

She checked in her tent,
no luck.

"Daddy! Bunny is missing!"

"Maybe Bunny is playing a game of hide-and-seek?" said Daddy.

"No! We do that together!" said Elle, sniffling.

"Why don't we go check in your bedroom," suggested Daddy.

When Elle walked into her room,
she saw a bunny sitting on her bed.

It looked like Bunny but when she picked it up
it didn't feel like Bunny.

"This isn't Bunny!" she yelled.

"But this looks just like Bunny," said Daddy.
"Maybe you two could play together and see how it goes?"

"Fine," said Elle. But she knew it wouldn't be the same.

She tried all afternoon to
play with this bunny.

This bunny was no good at
playing dress-up and didn't
even like tea parties.

This bunny wasn't even good at giving snuggles.

Suddenly Elle realized something. "I can't go to sleep without Bunny!"

Elle felt her insides tighten. She shook the bad thoughts away.

But nighttime had come quickly.

"I have never slept without Bunny!
I need Bunny to snuggle me to sleep." Elle sobbed to Daddy.

Just then Mommy walked in the front door.
She saw the tears rolling down Elle's cheeks.

"Why are you so sad, my love?"
she asked.

"Bunny is missing!" Elle cried.

"Oh no! Daddy didn't see the
note I left?" exclaimed Mommy.

Mommy smiled and grabbed Elle's hand.
"Come with me. I have a surprise for you."

Mommy walked Elle to the laundry room.

"Why don't you open the dryer," suggested Mommy.

"Bunny!"

She snuggled Bunny close to her. It felt just like Bunny.

"Wait a minute!" Elle yelled. "Something is different."

Bunny didn't smell stinky. Bunny smelled good!

Elle giggled, "Bunny, were you taking a bath today?"

Elle's heart filled with joy as she snuggled Bunny tight.

"I love you, Bunny!"

And Bunny was there to snuggle her, right to sleep.

For my daughter, Elle, with love.
May you never be too old for snuggles.
—RB

About the Author:

Renee Bolla, retail executive turned children's picture book writer. After 20 successful years in corporate retail Renee made the decision to resign. She resigned from pushing herself to climb higher up the corporate ladder in exchange for the freedom to slow down and find purpose. As a mother of three strong and talented daughters, she wanted to be more present, spend more time with family and discover more about herself. She has always been a curious human and creativity has always filled her soul. With the luxury of time and space to let her creative mind wander, she decided to explore writing. This journey started with the idea of creating a keepsake book for each of her children. Each story being unique to their personalities and real life experiences. While it started as a hobby, it has evolved in to much more. So here she is, a self-taught writer who is inspired by motherhood. It is the beginning of her writing journey and she is looking forward to sharing her stories with you.

@reneebollaauthor
www.reneebollaauthor.com

About the Illustrator:

Jess Bircham has been illustrating children's books for the past 10 years. She is most comfortable with a pencil in her hand and a sketchbook full of her fun and whimsical characters. Jess was raised in Bath, England, and much of her art is inspired by her early years growing up in the English countryside. She is a mother of two incredibly gifted boys and lives in a storybook log cabin in the mountains of Washington state, USA, with her husband, children, horses, dogs, cats and chickens! Jess has a passion for animals and nature and loves to spend time outdoors and riding her horses.

@jessbirchamillustration

Renee Bolla
www.reneebolllaauthor.com
ISBN: 978-0-578-36537-4 (Hardcover)

Design by Ashley Halsey
Illustrations Copyright © 2022 by Jess Bircham
First printing edition 2022
Printed in the U.S.A.

CPSIA information can be obtained
at www.ICGtesting.com
Printed in the USA
LVHW072103010422
714606LV00037B/1052